Freddy's Teddy

by Clare De Marco

Illustrated by Melanie Sharp

Crabtree Publishing Company

www.crabtreebooks.com

Crabtree Publishing Company

www.crabtreebooks.com
1-800-387-7650

616 Welland Ave.
St. Catharines, ON
L2M 5V6

PMB 59051, 350 Fifth Ave.
59th Floor,
New York, NY

Published by Crabtree Publishing in 2011

Series Editor: Jackie Hamley
Editor: Reagan Miller
Series Advisors: Dr. Hilary Minns, Catherine Glavina
Series Designer: Peter Scoulding
Project Coordinator: Kathy Middleton
Print and production coordinator: Katherine Berti

Text © Clare De Marco 2010
Illustration © Melanie Sharp 2010

Printed in Canada / 042011 / KR20110304

First published in 2010
by Franklin Watts
(A division of Hachette
Children's Books)

The rights of the author and the
illustrator of this Work have
been asserted.

**Library and Archives Canada
Cataloguing in Publication**

De Marco, Clare
    Freddy's teddy / by Clare De Marco ; illustrated by
Melanie Sharp.

(Tadpoles)
ISBN 978-0-7787-0577-2 (bound).--
ISBN 978-0-7787-0588-8 (pbk.)

    I. Sharp, Melanie II. Title. III. Series: Tadpoles
(St. Catharines, Ont.)

PZ7.D437Fr 2011   j823'.92   C2011-900152-7

**Library of Congress
Cataloging-in-Publication Data**

De Marco, Clare.
    Freddy's teddy / by Clare De Marco ; illustrated by
Melanie Sharp.
        p. cm. -- (Tadpoles)
    Summary: Little Teddy has a rip, but Freddy's mother has
needle, thread, and more than enough stuffing to fix him.
    ISBN 978-0-7787-0588-8 (pbk. : alk. paper) --
    ISBN 978-0-7787-0577-2 (reinforced library binding :
alk. paper)
    [1. Teddy bears--Fiction. 2. Sewing--Fiction.] I. Sharp,
Melanie, ill. II. Title. III. Series.

PZ7.D33958Fre 2011
[E]--dc22
                                                2010052362

Here is a list of the words in this story.
Common words:

a	had	Mom	she	too
big	him	no	some	will
but	I	oh	the	
can	into	put	then	
got	little	said	to	

Other words:

bed	fixed	much	Teddy
call	Freddy	rip	used
fix	hospital	stuffing	

Little Teddy had a rip.

"Oh no!" said Freddy.

4

"To the hospital,"
said Mom.

Mom put Little Teddy into bed.

Then she got
some stuffing.

"I can fix him,"
said Mom.

Mom fixed Little Teddy.

14

15

But she used too much stuffing!

16

18

"I will call him Big Teddy!"
said Freddy.

Puzzle Time

Can you find these pictures in the story?

c

d

Which pages are
the pictures from?

Turn over for the answers!

Answers

The pictures come from these pages:
a. pages 16 and 17
b. pages 20 and 21
c. pages 4 and 5
d. pages 14 and 15

Notes for adults

Tadpoles are structured to provide support for early readers. The stories may also be used by adults for sharing with young children.

Starting to read alone can be daunting. **Tadpoles** help by listing the words in the book for a preview before reading. **Tadpoles** also provide strong visual support and repeat words and phrases. These books will both develop confidence and encourage reading and rereading for pleasure.

If you are reading this book with a child, here are a few suggestions:

1. Make reading fun! Choose a time to read when you and the child are relaxed and have time to share the story.

2. Look at the picture on the front cover and read the blurb on the back cover. What might the story be about? Why might the child like it?

3. Look at the list of words on page two. Can the child identify most of the words?

4. Encourage the child to retell the story using the jumbled picture puzzle on pages 22-23.

5. Discuss the story and see if the child can relate it to his or her own experiences, or perhaps compare it to another story he or she knows.

6. Give praise! Children learn best in a positive environment.

If you enjoyed this book, why not try another **TADPOLES** story?
Please see the back cover for more **TADPOLES** titles.
Visit **www.crabtreebooks.com** for other **Crabtree** books.